A Life In Pictures
Lady Gaga

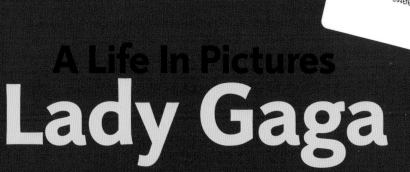

Marie Clayton

Trans
Atlantic
Press

Lady Gaga hit the music scene in 2006; young Stefani Germanotta chose a stage name based on The Queen hit 'Radio Ga Ga'.

Unusual and provocative ...'

A talented musician, Stefani had begun playing the piano at four and by her early teens was writing her own material and appearing at open mike nights. By 17 she had gained early admission to the prestigious Tisch School of the Arts in New York – one of only 20 students to do so – although she soon dropped out to pursue her musical career. She founded her first band, the Stefani Germanotta Band, or SGBand, which quickly gained a loyal fan base, but by mid-2006 had disbanded. Stefani began to work with music producer Rob Fusari and by September 2006 the newly incarnated Lady Gaga's 'unusual and provocative' performances had led to a recording contract with Def Jam Recordings – though the label dropped her after only three months.

Left and below: At the 2007 Lollapalooza festival, Chicago.

'The Ultimate Pop Burlesque Rockshow'

Having more fun

Above: Lady Gaga goes blonde for a performance with Lady Starlight (Colleen Martin) in October 2007. Being let go without having released a single record was devastating – but Lady Gaga soon moved on, beginning to explore the world of burlesque and go-go dancing in the underground nightlife culture of New York's Lower East Side. Gaga began appearing with performance artist Lady Starlight in a live art piece entitled 'Lady Gaga and the Starlight Revue', which was billed as 'The Ultimate Pop Burlesque Rockshow'. After working the New York downtown club circuit they were invited to play the 2007 Lollapalooza music festival at Grant Park in Chicago in August, where their performance was critically acclaimed.

Opposite: Performing at the Open A.I.R. Summer Concert Series in May 2008.

By the end of 2007 Gaga had a new label: Vincent Herbert had signed her to his newly created Streamline Records. Gaga later said of the deal with Herbert, 'I really feel like we made pop history, and we're gonna keep going.'

Debut single

Above: 'Just Dance' was recorded at the Record Plant studios in Hollywood and released in April 2008. To support her debut single Gaga performed regularly in clubs around the United States, as well as in various venues overseas. Here she performs in New York on May 15, 2008. 'Just Dance' was soon topping the charts in Australia, Canada, the Netherlands, the United Kingdom and the United States, and was nominated for a Grammy award in the Best Dance Recording category.

Opposite: Gaga also quickly became famous for her unusual, eye-catching and sometimes eccentric clothes, hair and make-up. In July 2008 she sported vivid pink streaks in her long blond hair – but this was only a mild indication of some of the more outrageous looks that were soon to come.

'Just Dance'

'That record saved my life. I was in such a dark space in New York. I was so depressed, always in a bar. I got on a plane to LA to do my music and was given one shot to write the song that would change my life and I did.'

'I want the imagery to be so strong that fans will want to eat and taste and lick every part of us.'

Style icon

The Origami Dress is one of Gaga's best-known outfits and has appeared in several versions. Here she is wearing it on stage while appearing as a supporting act on the New Kids on the Block reunion tour in 2008. Gaga has said that fashion is a major influence on her life and that when she is writing music she is thinking about the clothes she wants to wear on stage: 'It's all about everything altogether – performance art, pop performance art, fashion. For me, it's everything coming together and being a real story that will bring back the super-fan. I want to bring that back. I want the imagery to be so strong that fans will want to eat and taste and lick every part of us.'

'Poker Face' topped the singles charts in almost every category, in almost every major music market across the world.

Breaking all records ...

In 2008 Lady Gaga was working on her debut album in Los Angeles. She said later in an interview with MTV that she had been developing the songs for two and a half years, but that half the album had been completed in just one week. *The Fame* was released in August 2008 and included the hits 'Just Dance' and 'Poker Face'. It sold over 15 million copies worldwide and earned her six Grammy nominations and two wins, and a record-breaking 13 MTV Video Music Awards nominations. She became the first artist in history to achieve four No. 1 hits from a debut album, with 'Just Dance', 'Poker Face', 'LoveGame' and 'Paparazzi' all hitting the top spot.

Above: On stage in San Jose, California, during the New Kids on the Block reunion tour in 2008.

'The music is intended to inspire people to feel a certain way about themselves'

Haus of Gaga

Lady Gaga's own creative team, Haus of Gaga, is responsible for the sets, costumes and make-up for her tours, as well as for other one-off creations that represent the Gaga style. 'I called all my coolest art friends and we sat in a room and I said that I wanted to make my face light up. Or that I wanted to make my cane light up. Or that I wanted to make a pair of dope sunglasses. Or that I want to make video glasses, or whatever it was that I wanted to do. It's a whole amazing creative process that's completely separate from the label ...'

Many of the songs on *The Fame* explored the love of fame in different ways – in a newspaper interview Gaga said: 'The music is intended to inspire people to feel a certain way about themselves, so they'll be able to encompass, in their own lives, a sense of inner fame that they can project to the world, and the carefree nature of the album is a reflection of that aura.'

Dressed to thrill

Above: The Crystal Glasses worn on stage at the New Year's Eve Ball in New York on December 31, 2008. These were the first glasses created by the Haus of Gaga in 2008, made of pierced acrylic with crushed acrylic crystals clustered over one lens. Gaga wears them on the cover of her debut album, *The Fame*, so they are also often known as the Fame Glasses. Later different versions were made for live performances because Gaga could not see properly through the originals. The glasses were often worn as part of a set that also included the Disco Stick and the Disco Glove.

Opposite: On stage with the Disco Stick at the Zenith in Germany in February 2009. This prop has essentially not been changed since its first appearance in clubs in 2008 and is often still used. It was designed by Gaga with her then creative director, Matthew Williams, and is a short silver or black pole topped with a cluster of crystals made of crushed acrylic that contain small LEDs to create a bright blue-white light.

The term 'Disco Stick' was first used as a catchphrase in a bar, as Gaga explained in an interview with *Rolling Stone* magazine: 'I was in a bar in New York and I said to this guy I was hitting on, "I wanna take a ride on your disco stick", and he just started laughing.' The next day, the phrase became the inspiration for the song 'LoveGame'.

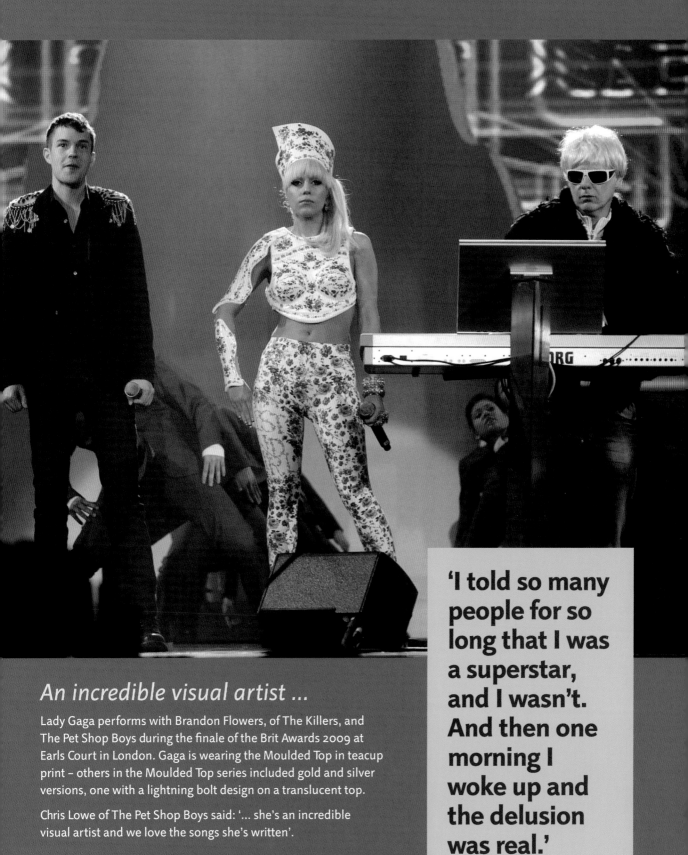

An incredible visual artist ...

Lady Gaga performs with Brandon Flowers, of The Killers, and The Pet Shop Boys during the finale of the Brit Awards 2009 at Earls Court in London. Gaga is wearing the Moulded Top in teacup print – others in the Moulded Top series included gold and silver versions, one with a lightning bolt design on a translucent top.

Chris Lowe of The Pet Shop Boys said: '... she's an incredible visual artist and we love the songs she's written'.

'I told so many people for so long that I was a superstar, and I wasn't. And then one morning I woke up and the delusion was real.'

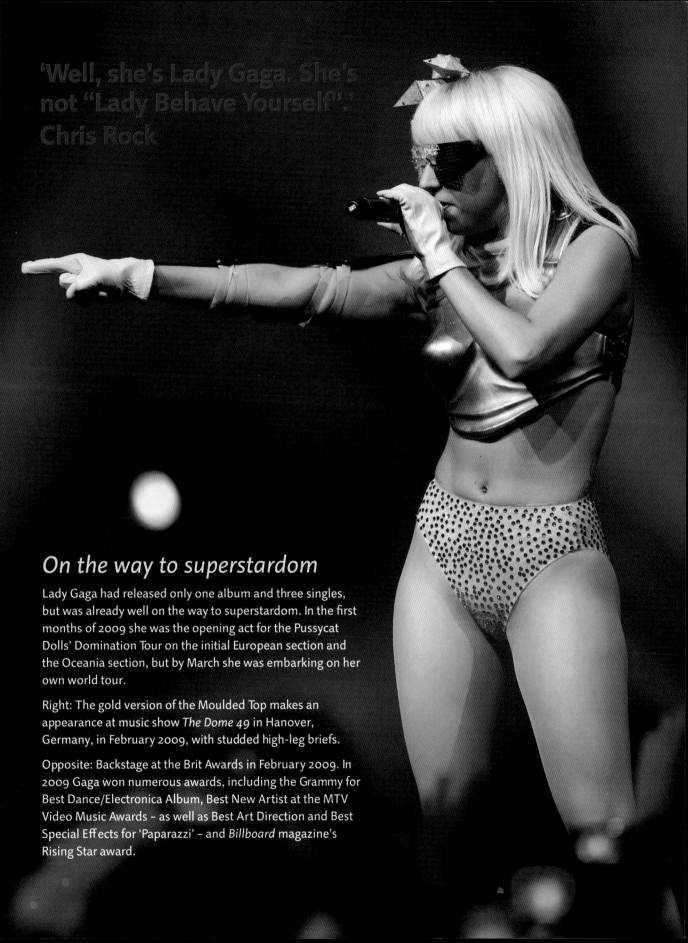

'Well, she's Lady Gaga. She's not "Lady Behave Yourself".'
Chris Rock

On the way to superstardom

Lady Gaga had released only one album and three singles, but was already well on the way to superstardom. In the first months of 2009 she was the opening act for the Pussycat Dolls' Domination Tour on the initial European section and the Oceania section, but by March she was embarking on her own world tour.

Right: The gold version of the Moulded Top makes an appearance at music show *The Dome 49* in Hanover, Germany, in February 2009, with studded high-leg briefs.

Opposite: Backstage at the Brit Awards in February 2009. In 2009 Gaga won numerous awards, including the Grammy for Best Dance/Electronica Album, Best New Artist at the MTV Video Music Awards – as well as Best Art Direction and Best Special Effects for 'Paparazzi' – and *Billboard* magazine's Rising Star award.

The Fame
Ball Tour

In March 2009 Gaga embarked
on her debut headlining tour, the
Fame Ball Tour, which opened
in San Diego and then travelled
around North America. By
May the tour had moved on to
Oceania, and in July and August
covered Europe and Asia. The
set list consisted mainly of tracks
from *The Fame*, and the four-
part show was designed in three
versions to suit different sizes
of venue. Critical reaction was
positive: Craig Rosen from the
Hollywood Reporter said: 'Lady
Gaga showed she's a serious
contender to Madonna's crown
Friday at the Wiltern. She might
be a relative newcomer, but
the artist born Stefani Joanne
Germanotta commanded the
stage with a royal air during
her hourlong set, at times even
sporting a glowing scepter.'

**'a serious contender to
Madonna's crown'**

**'The girl can, and does, sing.'
Entertainment Weekly**

The Hair Bow, an accessory made of hair, created by Gaga with Patricia Morales.

Not really a tour, more of a travelling party ...

For the opening song on the Fame Ball Tour Lady Gaga appears on stage from the centre of a ring of mirrored shields held by her dancers, wearing the Mirrored Dress and singing 'Paparazzi'. The dress is largely black, with hand rests built into the skirt, and two large mirror-mosaic triangular segments on the bodice and peplum. Latter versions of the dress included one completely covered in mirror shards and another in plain black. Critics commented on Gaga's fearless fashion sense – but also reported that she pulled off the theatrical set pieces 'like a seasoned pro'.

'I want it to be an entire experience from [the] minute you walk in [the] front door to [the] minute I begin to sing. And when it's all over, everyone's going to press rewind and relive it again.'

By the end of 2009, 'Just Dance' had sold three million copies in the United States alone. The single went on to go six-times platinum in both the US and Canada.

Blowing bubbles ...

Inspired by a dress created by Hussein Chalayan for his Spring 2007 show, the Bubble Dress was designed by the Haus of Gaga for the Fame Ball Tour. Gaga wears it while playing a glass piano filled with bubbles to debut a new song, 'Future Love', during the second part of the early shows on the tour. For the later European leg 'Brown Eyes' replaced 'Future Love' and the dress was replaced with a bubble vest, which was easier to remove for costume changes.

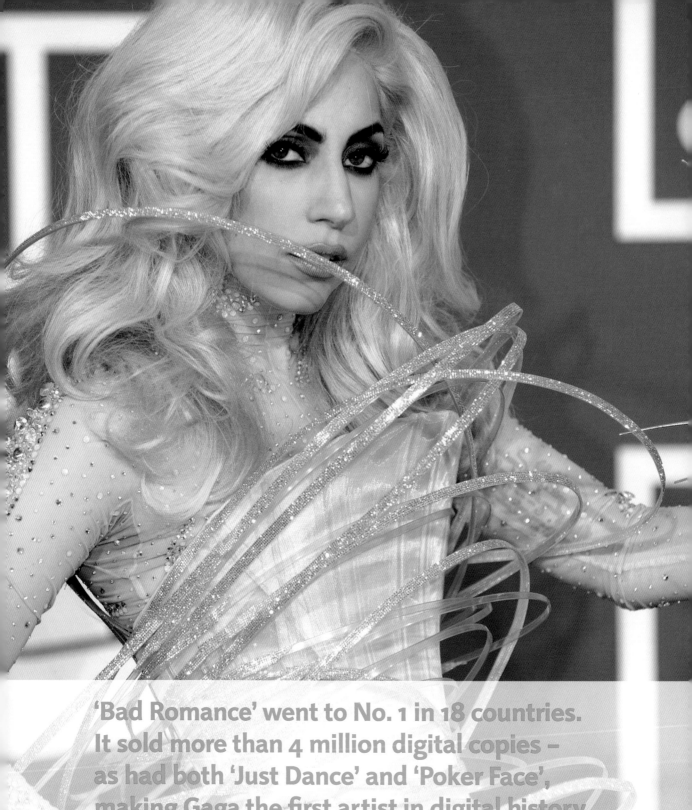

'Bad Romance' went to No. 1 in 18 countries.
It sold more than 4 million digital copies –
as had both 'Just Dance' and 'Poker Face',
making Gaga the first artist in digital history
to have achieved this three times.

The Fame Monster

The theme of the new EP was the darker side of fame, now that Gaga had personal experience of it. Originally *The Fame Monster* was to be released as a set with a re-release of *The Fame*, but Gaga decided the concepts were too different. However, a double set was later released, which included additional items, such as a lock from one of Gaga's wigs. 'Bad Romance', the lead single from *The Fame Monster*, was released in October 2009.

Opposite: Lady Gaga arriving at the 52nd Grammy Awards in Los Angeles on January 31, 2010, where she was to receive the award for Best Dance Single for 'Poker Face', beating both Madonna and Britney Spears. 'Poker Face' had also been nominated for both Song of the Year and Record of the Year.

Right: As a MAC Viva Glam spokesperson, a 'snow'-encrusted Lady Gaga arrives a benefit at Cipriani, New York, in February 2010. MAC donated 100 per cent of the proceeds from Viva Glam lip products to fight HIV and AIDS – the sales of Viva Glam Gaga lipstick and lip gloss alone raised more than $202 million.

The Monster Ball Tour was a huge success, with sold-out shows. Over its 18-month run Gaga played to an estimated 2.5 million fans.

'A meticulously choreographed spectacle ...'

The Monster Ball Tour, a new tour to promote *The Fame Monster,* had begun in Montreal, Canada, on November 27, 2009 – only two months after the Fame Ball Tour had drawn to a close on September 29 in Washington D.C. The initial dates on the new tour featured a frame set, and the show was based on a theme of human evolution, but as the tour moved into 2010 the theme was revised to tell a story of Gaga and her friends lost in New York City as they tried to travel to the Monster Ball. The show was in five parts, with short videos dividing each section. Aidin Vaziri from the *San Francisco Chronicle* called the original version 'not so much a live concert as a meticulously choreographed spectacle', while Kelly Nestruck of the *Guardian* thought, 'Lady Gaga's "electro-pop opera" is at least twice as entertaining and infinitely fresher than any stage musical written over the last decade.'

Left: While in Japan for the Monster Ball Tour in April 2010, Lady Gaga appeared at a charity concert in Tokyo for people living with HIV.

'A 40-foot animatronic sea monster, 15 costume changes and a grand piano burning to pieces in the middle of the stage – you certainly get what you pay for at a Lady Gaga concert.'

Working for others...

Above: Debbie Harry and Lady Gaga performing at the Rainforest Fund's 21st birthday at Carnegie Hall, New York City, in May 2010. Gaga has been involved with various charities and fund-raising efforts – she donated the entire proceeds of a concert at Radio City Music Hall in New York to the Haiti reconstruction relief fund, and designed a Japan Prayer Bracelet to benefit relief efforts after the Japanese tsunami in 2011. In 2011 she also launched the Born This Way Foundation, which supports young people facing bullying and abandonment.

Opposite: The Monster Ball plays the O2 Arena in London. The revised show was more ambitious in scope than the original, even though it was put together in only four weeks. One of the emotional high points of the show was the performance of 'Speechless', a song that was written by Gaga partly in response to her father's illness.

'There's an immense emotional intelligence behind the way she uses her voice. Almost never does she overwhelm a song with her vocal ability, recognizing instead that artistry is to be found in nuance rather than lung power.'

Although Lady Gaga has only been performing for a few years, she is constantly reinventing herself and her music. She has often been compared to artists such as Madonna or Gwen Stefani, partly because of her ability to cause controversy and also because of her vocal range, which spans 2.4 octaves. However, most critics agree that she has a distinctive style and is a truly talented and original musician.

Health warning ...

During 2010 it was revealed that Lady Gaga had tested borderline positive for lupus, news that dismayed her fans. However, she assured them that she was not affected by any symptoms and in an interview with David Letterman said that she planned to avoid future problems with diet and a healthy lifestyle. Her aunt, Joanne Germanotta, died of lupus aged only 19.

Gaga wears a translucent nun's habit and a skeletal hand while performing at the 2010 Lollapalooza music festival in Grant Park in Chicago. The outfit was designed for the Monster Ball Tour – on the tour she wore it to sing 'LoveGame' inside a gilded subway carriage, during the Subway section of the show.

Opposite: Another costume from Lollapalooza 2010: a purple cheetah-print leotard with fishnets worn under a purple leather jacket with huge crystal-encrusted shoulder pads. Accessories included purple jewelled shades, heavily cropped leather gloves and bright yellow hair extensions.

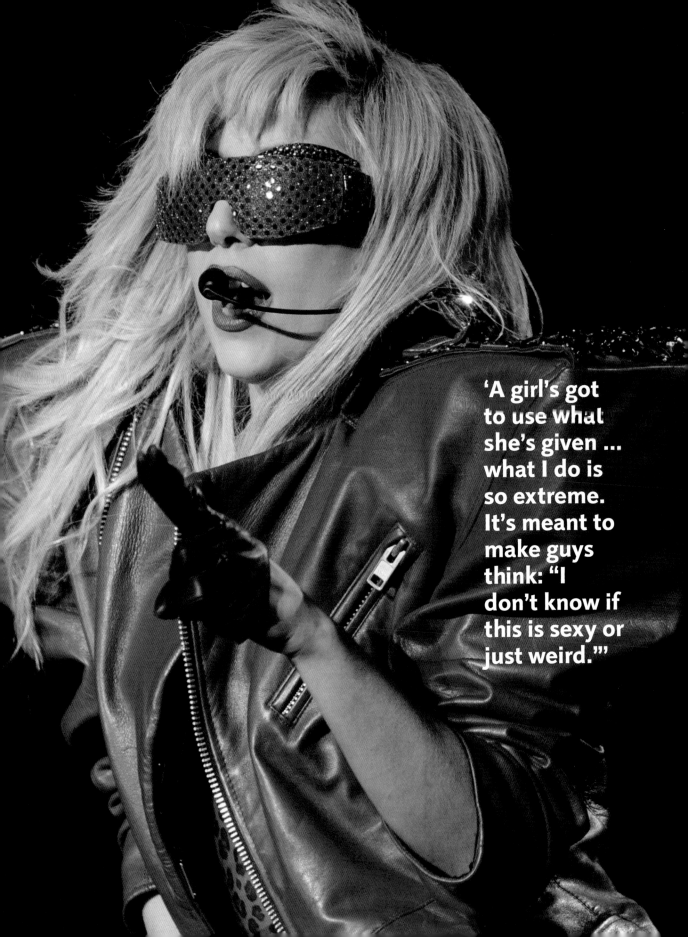

'A girl's got
to use what
she's given ...
what I do is
so extreme.
It's meant to
make guys
think: "I
don't know if
this is sexy or
just weird."'

Well-dressed meat...

To accept the Video of the Year
award at the MTV video awards
in 2010, Gaga wore a dress made
entirely of raw meat, designed
by Franc Fernandez. It caused a
sensation: condemned by PETA and
the Vegetarian Society and voted the
major fashion statement of 2010 by
Time magazine. Later on *The Ellen
DeGeneres Show* – to which she wore
the dress again – Gaga said, '... it
has many interpretations. For me
this evening, if we don't stand up for
what we believe in and if we don't
fight for our rights pretty soon, we're
going to have as much rights as the
meat on our own bones. And, I am
not a piece of meat.'

Between appearances the Meat Dress was frozen to prevent it deteriorating, but was then preserved by taxidermist Sergio Vigilato – who turned it into a type of beef jerky. In 2011 it went on display in the Rock and Roll Hall of Fame.

The single 'Born This Way' made it to No. 1 in 18 countries. It also broke records for digital downloads, selling a million copies worldwide on iTunes in just five days, and nearly four million in the United States alone by the end of 2011.

Born this way...

In February 2011 'Bad Romance' picked up its eighth award when it won a Grammy for Best Short Form Music Video. The awards ceremony also marked the debut live performance of 'Born This Way' – the first single from the forthcoming album of the same name – which had shot to the No. 1 spot in the *Billboard* Hot 100 on its release two days earlier. Written in Liverpool, England, during the Monster Ball Tour, Gaga said the song was based on the idea that who you are when you are first born is not necessarily who you will become – that you have your whole life to make yourself into who you want to be.

Right: Arriving at the *Late Show* with David Letterman in May 2011 shortly after the release of her second studio album, *Born This Way*, which debuted at the top spot in the *Billboard* 200 chart and had sold more than a million copies within the first few days.

Opposite: Spotted out and about in New York, Lady Gaga sports vivid green hair.

Gaga meets Bollywood ...

Left: Sporting a hairdo in the colours of the Indian flag and an asymmetrical gown by Indian-American designer Naeem Khan at a press conference in October 2011, before a performance at the after-party for India's first Formula One Grand Prix. Gaga hinted her outfit for the show would be a 'hybrid of my vision and the Indian vision'. She appeared in a brief PVC-style skirt that wrapped around her thighs over a bejewelled leotard, with a sweeping white veil, huge beaded choker and towering black PVC heels.

Gaga is also a star in the social networking world, with over 33 million 'likes' on Facebook, and is at No. 1 on Twitter with over 13 million followers.

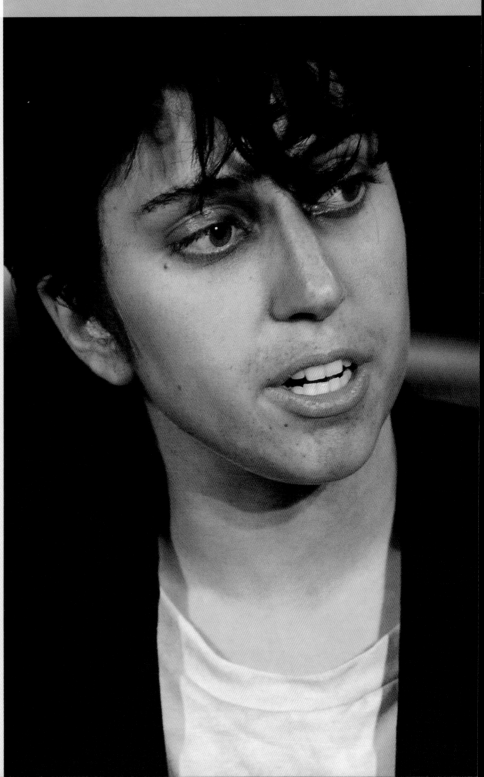

A male alter ego

Right: Gaga attended the 2011 MTV Video Music Awards as 'Jo Calderone', who had been created in June 2010 for a men's fashion editorial for *Vogue Hommes Japan*. Photographs of Jo, with slicked-back dark hair, were released after the shoot, announcing he was a newly discovered male model, but rumours quickly began that 'he' was really Gaga – which was confirmed during an interview that August. Black and white photos of Jo Calderone, sporting sideburns and a cigarette, feature on the cover of the fourth single from *Born This Way*, 'Yoü and I', released in August 2011. At the MTV awards Jo performed a monologue and sang 'Yoü and I' on the piano before doing a dance routine and ending the song with Brian May. For the two days leading up to the performance, Gaga became Jo Calderone, so her portrayal would be convincing.

In June 2011, *Rolling Stone* magazine ranked 16 solo female artists, looking at album and digital song sales, Hot 100 rankings, radio airplay, YouTube views, social media, concert grosses, industry awards and critics' ratings. As a result they named Lady Gaga the Queen of Pop.

Right: Performing her hit single 'Judas' at a waterfront concert at the Cannes Film Festival, France, in May 2011. With the Mediterranean Sea as her backdrop, Gaga treated thousands of fans to a memorable, high-energy performance, accompanied by a retinue of male dancers.

In November she released 'Marry the Night', the fifth single from *Born This Way*, which was inspired by Gaga's love of partying and of her home town, New York. She recorded a special version of the song for her Thanksgiving Day television special, *A Very Gaga Thanksgiving*, which aired on ABC in the United States on November 24, 2011. Tony Bennett, with whom Gaga sang 'The Lady is a Tramp' on the show, said he saw 'a touch of theatrical genius' in her, that 'she might become America's Picasso'.

Award winner

Opposite: At the MTV Europe Music Awards, held in Belfast, Northern Ireland, Lady Gaga had six nominations and won in four categories: Best Female and Biggest Fans, and – for 'Born This Way' – Best Song and Best Video.

This page: Lady Gaga is naturally a brunette, but went blonde in 2007 – apparently because she was often mistaken for Amy Winehouse. Since then her hair has frequently been vividly coloured and she has created many extraordinary hairstyles for her shows and for personal appearances.

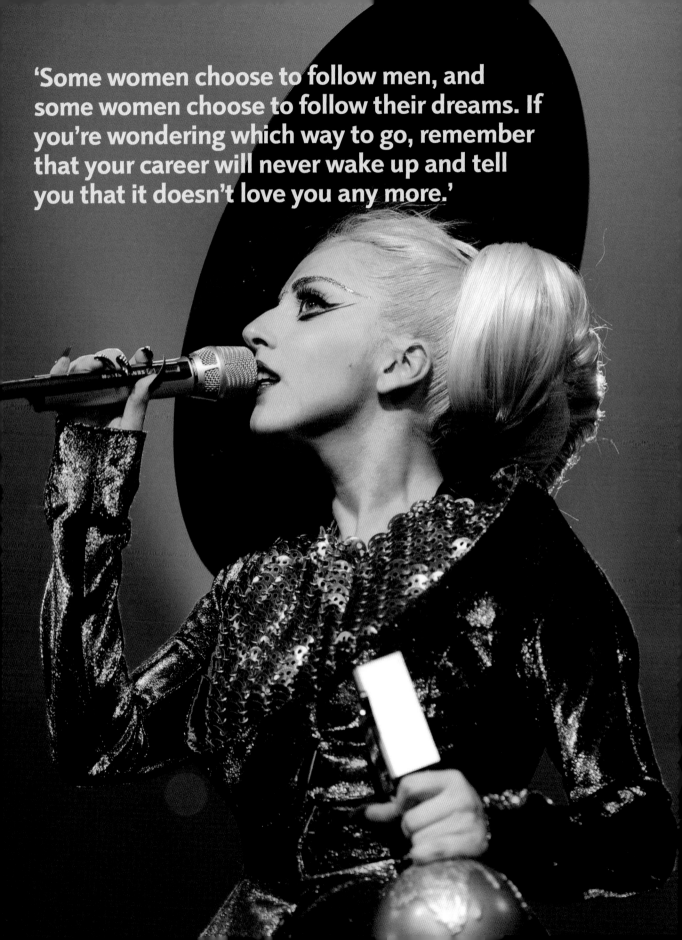

'Some women choose to follow men, and some women choose to follow their dreams. If you're wondering which way to go, remember that your career will never wake up and tell you that it doesn't love you any more.'

Meteoric career

Left: Lady Gaga on stage at Madison Square Garden in her home town of New York. On December 31, 2011, she also performed at New York's famous Times Square New Year celebrations, which are broadcast live across America (opposite). Just before midnight she joined NYC Mayor Bloomberg for the historic countdown in front of an estimated crowd of one million.

Gaga's contributions to the music industry have brought her numerous awards in her meteoric career, including five Grammy awards from twelve nominations, two Guinness world records and the estimated sales of 15 million albums and 51 million singles worldwide. She has been included in *Time* magazine's annual '*Time* 100' list of the most influential people in the world and in *Forbes* magazine's lists of the 'World's Most Powerful Celebrities' and the world's '100 Most Powerful Women' – on which she made it to No. 7. In an interview she once said: 'I had a boyfriend who told me I'd never succeed, never be nominated for a Grammy, never have a hit song, and that he hoped I'd fail. I said to him, "Someday, when we're not together, you won't be able to order a cup of coffee at the deli without hearing or seeing me."' And she was right.

This is a Transatlantic Press book
First published in 2012

Transatlantic Press
38 Copthorne Road
Croxley Green, Hertfordshire
WD3 4AQ, UK

Text © Transatlantic Press
Images © Getty Images

A catalogue record for this book is available from the British Library.
ISBN 978-1-908533-98-2

Printed in China